Fuzz, the Famous Fly

Written by Emily Rodda
Illustrated by Tom Jellett

An easy-to-read SOLO
for beginning readers

SOLOS

Southwood Books Limited
4 Southwood Lawn Road
London N6 5SF

First published in Australia by Omnibus Books 1999

Published in the UK under licence from
Omnibus Books by
Southwood Books Limited, 2000.

This edition produced for The Book People Ltd.,
Hall Wood Avenue, Haydock, St Helens WA11 9UL

Text copyright © Emily Rodda 1999
Illustrations copyright © Tom Jellett 1999

Cover design by Lyn Mitchell

ISBN 1 903207 09 6

Printed in Hong Kong

A CIP catalogue record for this book is available
from the British Library

For Peter Bateman,
Fuzz's first photographer – E.R.

For Chloe, Bianca and Celine – T.J.

Chapter 1

Fuzz was very good-looking, for a fly. His eyes sparkled like stars. His wings were as shiny as rain on broken glass. His legs were long and thin, and he kept them very clean.

He was also clever, and good at singing and dancing.

Fuzz lived in a small park with his friends and family.

Their home was a cosy rubbish bin near a picnic bench. There was always lots of excellent rubbish in the bin, and it had a beautiful view of the gutter.

One morning, Fuzz was having
breakfast – rotten hamburger with
squashed banana on top – when
some visitors came into the park
and sat on the bench.

The man's shirt was the colour of
very old cheese. He was carrying
a camera.

The woman wore bright green clothes, and Fuzz could see that she had eaten toast and honey for breakfast. Crumbs were sticking to the front of her dress.

Fuzz loved toast and honey. He
was sure the woman didn't want
the crumbs. So he went and helped
himself.

The man lifted the camera, and the woman smiled.

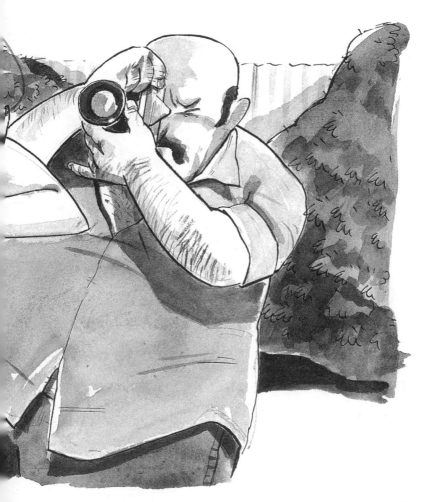

"That's nice," said Fuzz to himself.
"She likes me." He did a little dance
and buzzed a song in the woman's
ear, to show that he liked her too.

The woman waved and clapped.
"Hold still," called the man, so
Fuzz did.

Click! The man took a picture.

Fuzz finished his toast and flew away, not knowing that this day was going to change his life.

Chapter 2

A few days later, the flies were having lunch – pizza mixed with peanut butter – when another visitor came into the park and sat on the bench.

He smelt wonderful, because he had trodden in something brown and sticky in the grass.

The visitor started to read the paper. All the flies went to look. They liked to see the news.

The man waved the paper at them.

"That's nice," Fuzz said. "He's trying to show it to us."

Soon the man muttered, "Flies!" and went away, leaving the paper lying on the bench.

"You heard what he said," Fuzz told his friends. "He's left it for us to see."

They all buzzed down to look at the paper. And there, on the open page, was a picture of the woman in the green dress – and Fuzz!

"Look!" buzzed all the flies. "Fuzz! You're in the paper! You're famous!"

Fuzz felt so shy that he went pink, which for a fly is quite difficult.

But that was only the beginning.

Chapter 3

Word spread fast. Soon all the flies in the park had seen the paper. Lots of them asked for Fuzz's autograph.

By lunch time, a fan club had started.

Many visitors came to the park
that day. The flies knew that they
had come because they had seen
Fuzz's picture in the paper.

Fuzz tried to say hello to every-one, so that no one felt left out. He danced and sang, too.

The visitors waved and clapped.
They loved him!

Fuzz was so busy that he hardly had time to eat. He missed at least six meals!

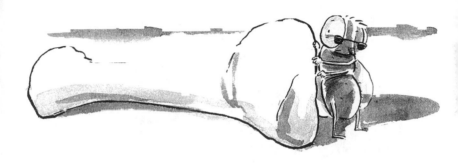

In the end, he had to rest. He put on sunglasses, so his fans wouldn't know him, and hid behind an old chicken bone.

The other flies came to visit him there. "Fuzz, you are a star," his wise old granny said. "You must leave home and share your talent with the world."

"Really?" said Fuzz. He was so excited that his tummy was flopping up and down. He ate some chicken, to settle it.

"Yes," agreed all the flies. "Fuzz, you are a star."

Fuzz felt very proud. "I'm a star," he said to himself.

He quickly packed a bag and buzzed out of the rubbish bin. A big car was waiting.

Fuzz took his place in the back
seat. Then the car drove away.

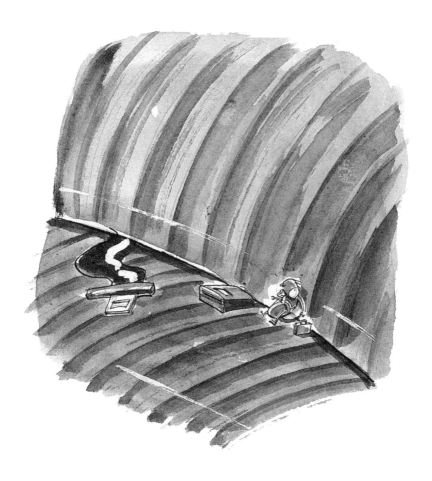

Fuzz pressed his nose against the window and watched until the little park was out of sight.

Chapter 4

Fuzz enjoyed life as a star. Everyone he met was very nice to him. They waved when they saw him, and clapped when he sang and danced. They loved him!

He worked hard. He was in ads and TV shows, and quite a few films.

His picture was often in the papers, too. He liked this best, because he knew that the flies at home would see the papers, and know he was OK.

He hoped they were proud of
him. He hadn't seen them for a very
long time. By now he had moved
around the city so much that he
no longer knew how to get back to
the park.

Fuzz was famous. He ate the best food and drank the best drinks.

He drove in big cars, and slept in the richest bins in the city.

But sometimes, late at night, when he was alone, he felt sad.

"I know I'm lucky to be famous," he said to himself. "But I miss the old flies at home."

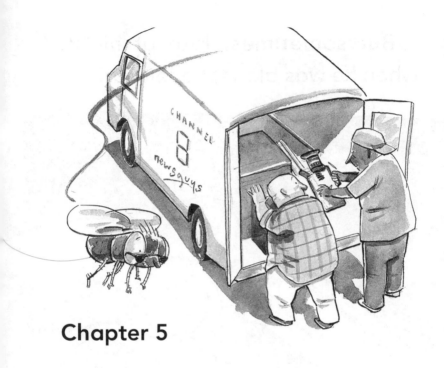

Chapter 5

One morning, Fuzz went to make a TV ad about rubbish. He knew a lot about rubbish, and was glad to have the chance to tell everyone how wonderful it was.

He had been to a big party the night before, and had stayed up late. He was tired when he crawled into the TV van.

"Sometimes, being a star is hard," he said to himself, as the van bumped along. He decided to have a little sleep.

He woke up when the van stopped.

"What a dump!" he heard one of the TV people say.

"This sounds like a nice place," said Fuzz to himself. He buzzed outside and looked around.

At first he didn't know where he was. And then, suddenly, his heart jumped.

It was his park! There was the gutter. There was the dear old bin. He was home!

"Fuzz! Oh, Fuzz!" His friends and family had seen him. They buzzed towards him. They crowded around him and hugged him.

"Flies!" said the TV people, waving and clapping.

"I know," shouted Fuzz. "Isn't it wonderful?"

"Oh, Fuzz, we have missed you,"
his old granny cried.

"I've missed you too," said Fuzz.
"So much!"

When the TV people left that day, Fuzz didn't go with them. He was sorry to say goodbye. He knew they must be sorry, too. But he loved his old home too much to leave it, ever again.

And he never did.

When his fans came to the park, he always sang and danced for them. They waved and clapped, so he knew they still loved him.

But every night, as he snuggled down in his cosy bin, he felt very, very lucky.

"It's good to be famous," he said to himself. "But it's even better to be happy. And even for a famous fly like me, there's no place like home."

Emily Rodda

At home I have a photograph with a fly right in the middle of it. The fly sat on the camera lens while the picture was taken, just as though it wanted to be a star.

On TV you often see a fly buzzing around, if the show is about the outdoors. There have been flies in magazine pictures, too. I had always thought it was a different fly every time. Now I've started to wonder. Flies all look the same to us. But maybe there are special flies who try their hardest to be famous. Just like Fuzz.

Tom Jellett

I usually work next to an open window. This is great on a sunny day because a nice breeze blows in to cool me down. The problem is that the breeze also blows my drawings off the table, and I end up chasing them around the room!

Flies get in through my open window, too. They buzz all over the place, walk over my biscuits, fall into my cup of tea, and make real pests of themselves.

I tried to use these flies as models for my drawings of Fuzz and his friends, but I couldn't get them to sit still for a second!

More Solos!

Dog Star
Janeen Brian and Ann James

The Best Pet
Penny Matthews and Beth Norling

Fuzz the Famous Fly
Emily Rodda and Tom Jellett

Cat Chocolate
Kate Darling and Mitch Vane

Jade McKade
Jane Carroll and Virginia Barrett

I Want Earrings
Dyan Blacklock and Craig Smith

What a Mess Fang Fang
Sally Rippin

Cocky Colin
Richard Tulloch and Stephen Axelsen